Oh My
I Can Fly !
The Birdie Story

Gigi Tell me the Birdie Story

Michele Gajdzis

Dedication:

This book is dedicated to my granddaughters Avery, Addyson and Skylar, whose courage, inspiration, and creativity continue to leave footprints on my heart.
To the Ambrosio family and the next generation to come. May you never forget that God created you to soar
with eagles.
To children in every home. May you discover how truly loved you are. This book is for you.

ACKNOWLEDGEMENTS

This Book is a collaborative achievement. Credit must be given where credit is due. For that reason I am deeply thankful to everyone who has prayed, encouraged and Inspired this story to be told.

Thank you Dear Lord for depositing this story in my heart over thirty years ago. Thank you for allowing it to be told for just a time as this. May the thoughts and meditations of my heart always be pleasing to you as Your unfolding message of love is revealed.

To my devoted husband, Randy. Thank you for standing faithfully beside me these last fifty-one years. My co-adventurer in life, whose quiet strength, unwavering support have kept me laughing as we journeyed together. Thank you for never saying "no" to my wild ideas and reminding me of the purpose behind this tale. Your support helped turn a quiet calling into a living reality.

To my beloved children, Lisa & Kenny Burns, Jason & Lisa Gajdzis. You are my greatest joy. This story was only a dream quietly hidden away until your love and encouragement gave me the courage to fly, bringing it to life. May you always remember to keep soaring.

To Rita Maurio, my dearest friend & co-laborer. Thank you for walking beside me through every page of this story. You are a force that would not stop until it was completed. Thank you for your continued support, honest feedback and brainstorming moments that made all the difference in seeing this completed. This story could not have been told without your insight, your prayers and your belief when I needed it the most. I am endlessly grateful for your giftings and honored to have created this with you.

Most importantly, I want to thank the team from Book Publishing Professionals. My heartfelt gratitude for your steadfast commitment to putting wings to this story. Thank you ,Jay Cooper, for seeing the end from the beginning. Your vision was far greater than I could think or imagine. You are a treasured gift from above who has captured the zeal of story telling that changes the heart in every child.

A special thank you to Rhea Howard. Your editorial guidance comes with a divine spirit of excellence. You remind me that stories are not written alone; they're built on the love and trust shared by those who share the vision. Thank you for seeing the vision and running the race with endurance to get this finished. Time will tell of the adventures you have yet to discover.

Finally my deepest appreication to the Illustration team . Your creativity and attention to detail added depth and vibrancy to every page. What an amazing team to work with. Thank you for tirelessly working to capture the essence of the story, bringing life where words alone never could. Thank you for all your patience with making changes that made this story come alive.

Blessings

Michele

Copyrights©2025 Michele Gajdzis
All rights reserved.

Dedication:

No part of this book may be reproduced, stored in a retrieval system, or transmitted in any form or by any means—electronic, mechanical, photocopying, recording, or otherwise—without the prior written permission of the author, except in the case of brief quotations embodied in critical articles or reviews.

Case ID: TXu2-461-828

Once upon a time, there was a little bird named Barry. Barry lived all alone in a cage on top of a mountain. He spent his days looking out, watching all the other birds fly high above his little head. He dreamed that one day he might fly too.

"I wish I could fly just like them," Barry sighed. His cage was tightly locked, and he had no feathers to help him soar. Every day he sat quietly and thought, "Oh, please help me fly."

One morning, a bird with radiant colors landed outside his cage. "Who are you?" asked Barry.

"I'm Wally Bird," his visitor replied. "Why do you look so sad?" " I want to fly like all the other birds, but I'm locked up, and I have no feathers," Barry explained.

Barry noticed Wally's feathers. They were dazzling. He wanted the same. "Someday," Barry thought. "Someday." Wally spoke up. "Do you know that you are an eagle and were created to soar?"

"An eagle ?" Really ?" Barry said in disbelief. "What does that mean ?" " Time will tell, time will tell," Wally responded as he flew off.

The next day, Wally returned with a gift for Barry.
A shiny blue feather with gold letters.
" What is this ?" Asked Barry.
" This is a Promise Feather", Wally told him.
"Wear it proudly."

Wally had become a good friend. One morning, he arrived With Barry's Final Feather.
"This is the last feather you will need."Wally said. Barry's heart swelled with excitement. But he still didn't know what the gold letters meant.

Barry woke up feeling lonely. He stared at his promise feathers and wondered if he'd ever fly.

Just then, Wally Appeared.
" Are you ready to fly?" He asked.
" I don't know how." Barry whispered.
"I think I will need to Practice"

Wally started to Cheer.
" Try first in your cage, go ahead, give it a try."
Wally waited for Barry to take his first try.
Then his second, now, his third.

"What's wrong?" I have all the feathers I need. Why can't I move?"
" I know who can help," Wally answered as he flew off.

Wally soon returned with an answer. " This is my friend Kenny Bird," Wally told Barry.
" He's an eagle just like you, and he's an excellent teacher." Barry liked Kenny Bird. He was strong and majestic. " I can teach you to fly," Kenny said." But you must listen carefully." I promise to listen," Barry said.

Kenny began Barry's first Lesson. Teaching him to flap His wings up and down." Up and down, Up and down, He coached. "Ugh." Barry moaned as he did what Kenny said."Don't give up, don't give up, " Kenny cheered.
Barry worked Hard.
Soon His wings grew very strong.

The Big Day had Come. Kenny and Wally come close. " Today's the day," Kenny announced.
" Let's go."
Barry moved to the edge of His cage. But fear stopped him.
" I can't get out! " It's locked, my cage is locked."Barry shouted.
His eyes filled with tears.
" Will I ever fly. Wally?" " Will I ever be free?"Wally calmly responded, "Time will tell, time will tell."

Barry watched Kenny & Wally fly off.
" I wonder where they went."
" Will they ever come back ?"

Days went By, Kenny and Wally were nowhere in sight. Suddenly! Barry looked up. He heard a sound in the distance." It's Wally and Kenny!" They're Back!" He cried. " But who is that with them ?"

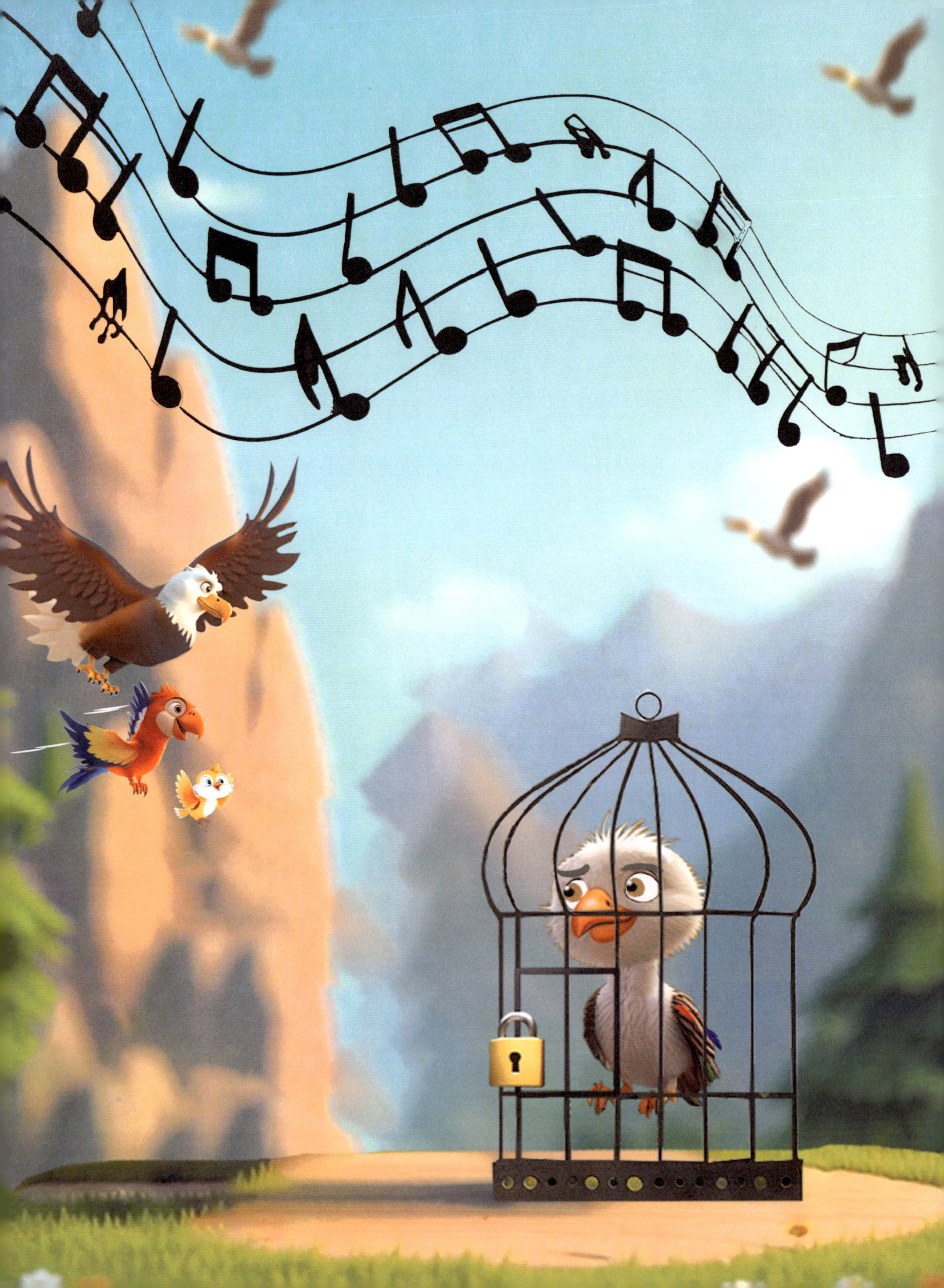

" Hi, Barry." Wally called out. " Did you miss us ?."" This is Harmony Bird. She's a singing bird."

" She sings songs that bring Joy, Hope & Strength," Wally said. Harmony began to sing a beautiful melody:" I got Hope, I got Strength, I got Joy…..OH Boy. !"
" I got Hope, I got Strength, I got Joy….. Oh Boy. !"Barry smiled, he loved Harmony, she made him so happy.But he wondered " How could Harmony's song help me to fly?" Time will Tell, Time will tell," he thought.

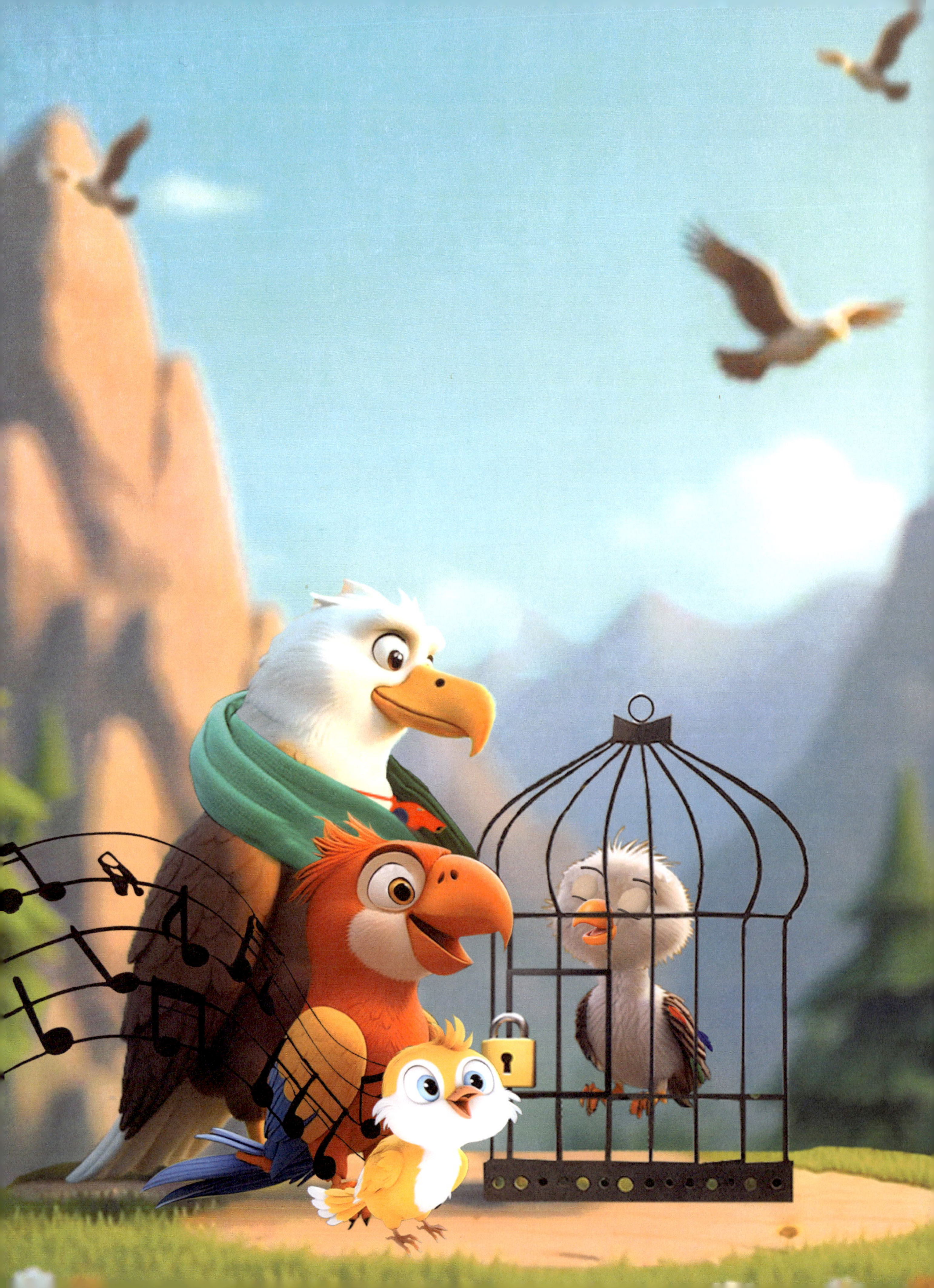

" Can you help Barry get free?" Wally asked Harmony. She nodded and started to sing even louder. Barry began singing along , as Joy filled his heart. All of Sudden, Something Amazing began to HAPPENED!

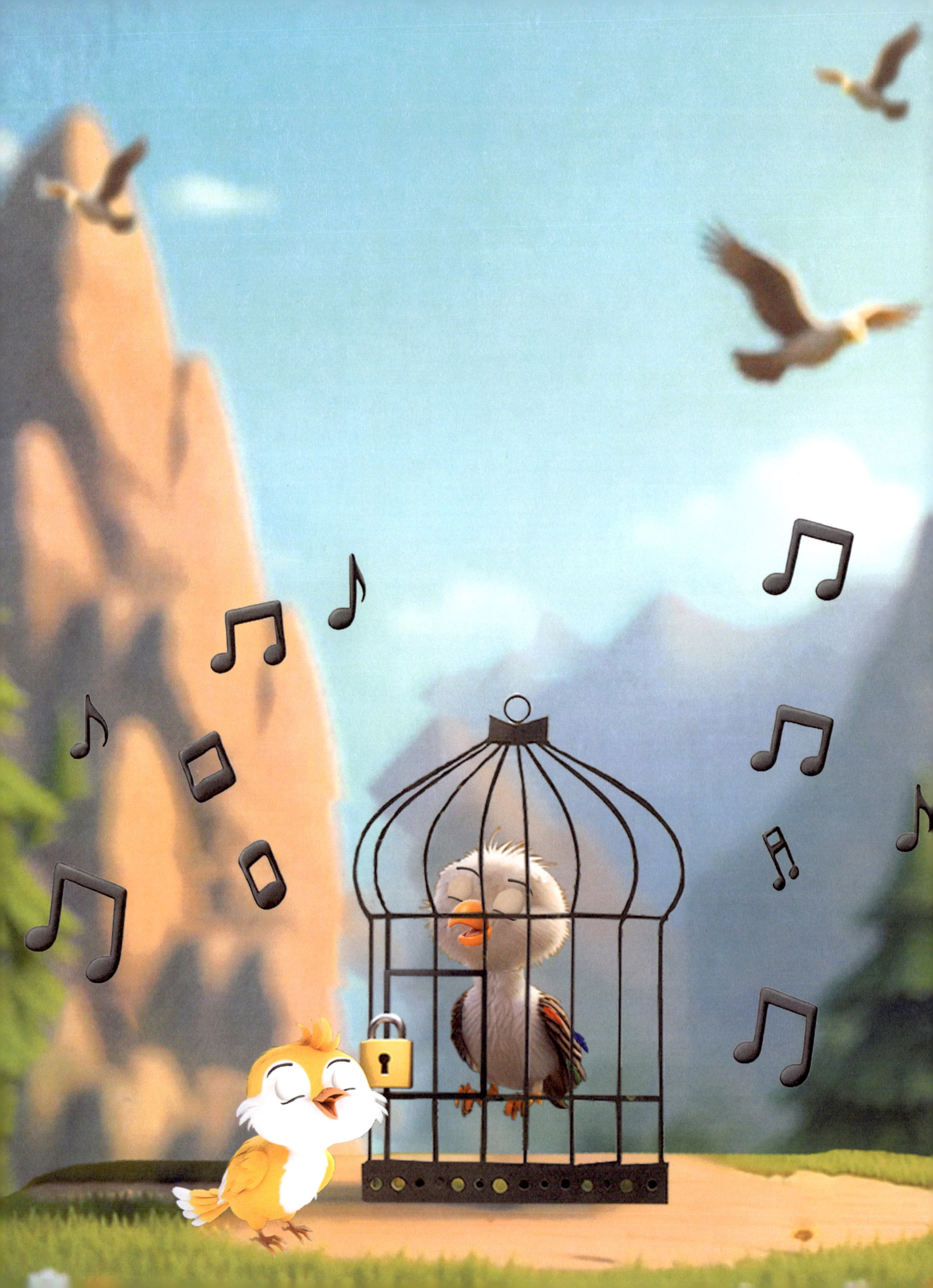

Barry's mountain began to SHAKE!
" WHAT'S HAPPENING!" Harmony sang out.
" DID YOU FEEL THAT. Barry ?"
" This has never happened before."He answered, Trying not to look nervous. Barry's cage began to sway back and forth. What happend next surprised everyone.

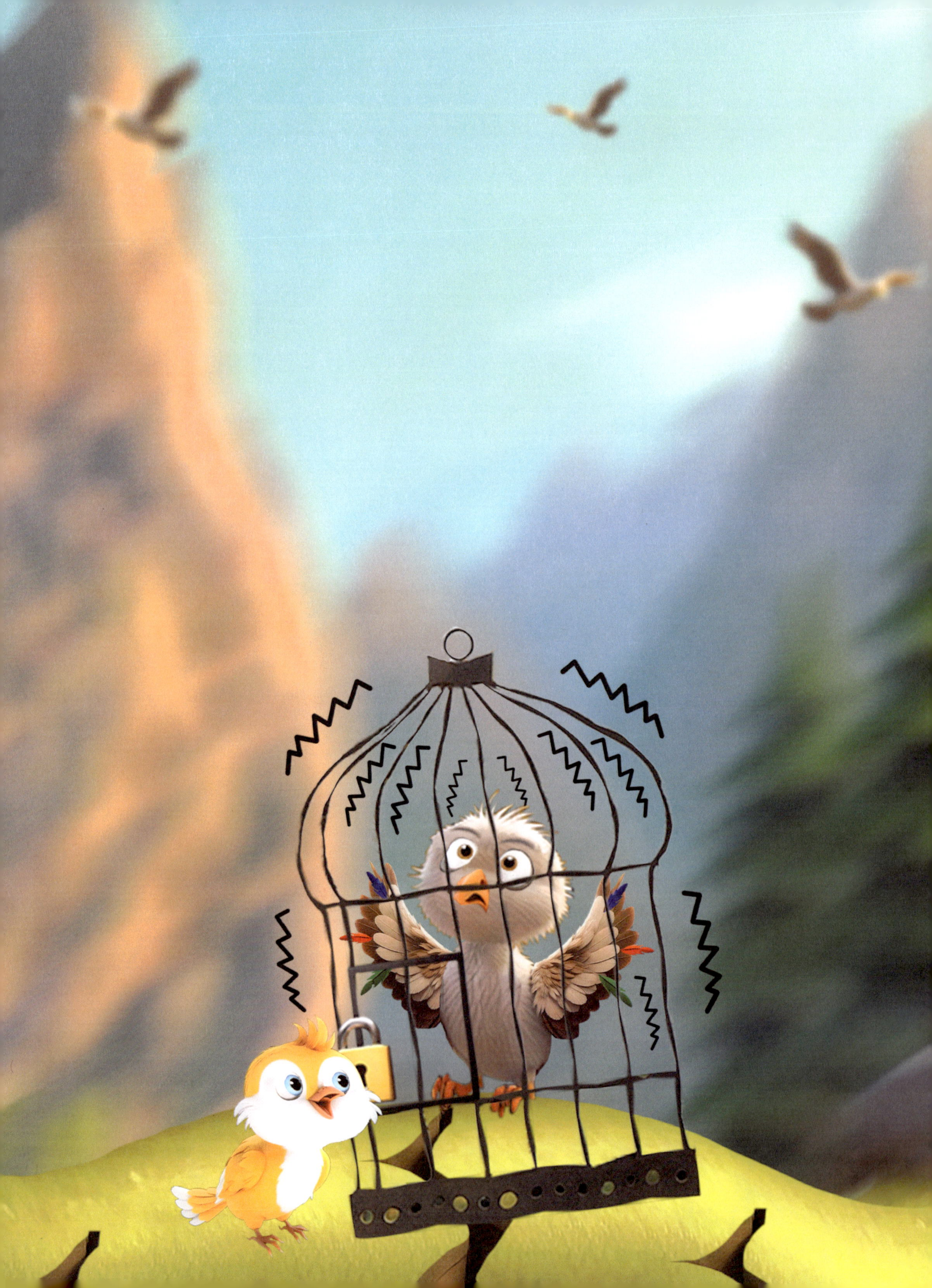

Suddenly! Barry's prision door broke open." Look !" His friends screamed." It's finished !" You're FREE!"
BARRY WAS FREE INDEED.
Now you are ready to fly? Wally announced.

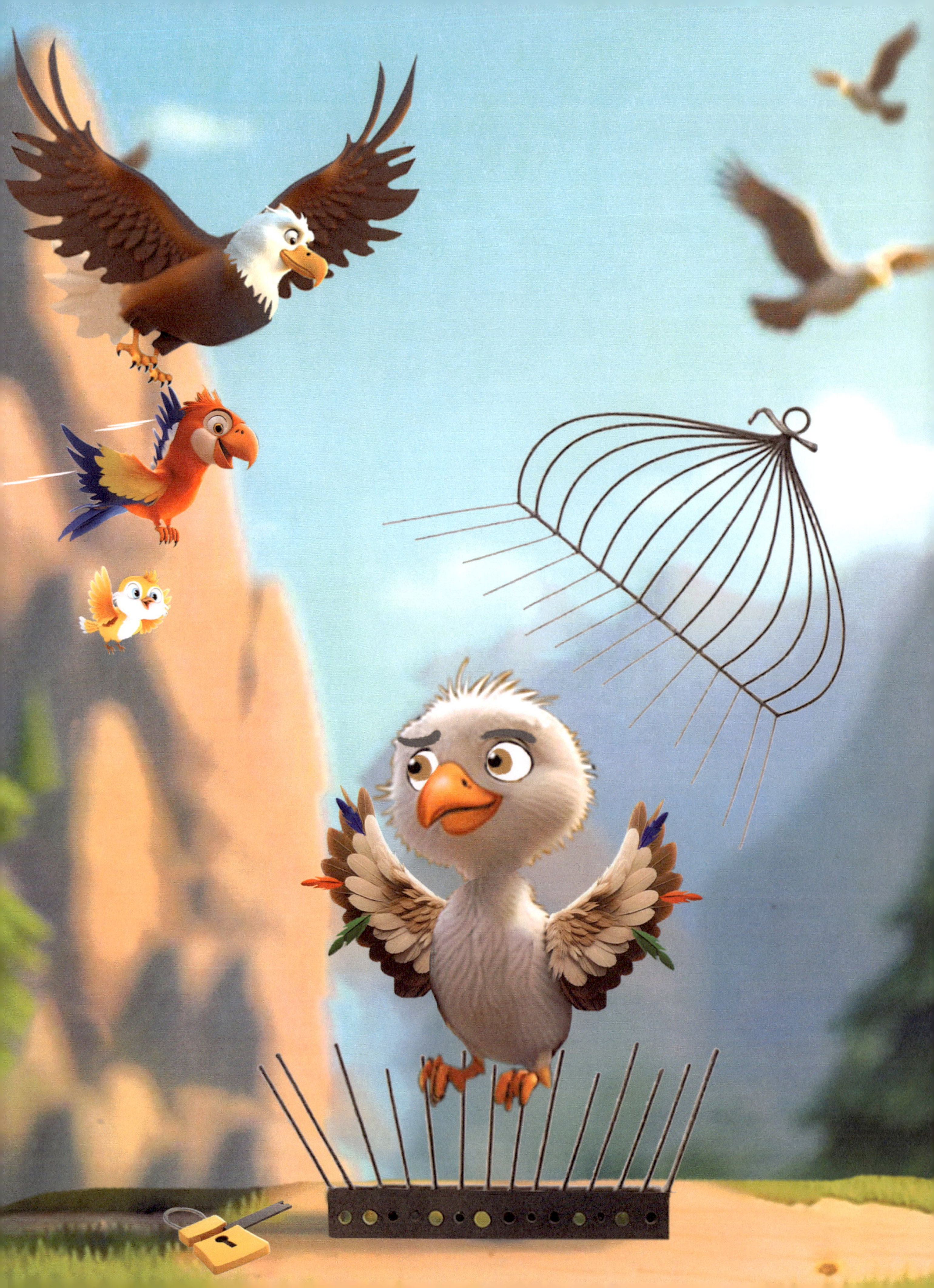

I'm scared", cried Barry. " I can't do this ," he told Wally. " Yes you can." Wally told the frightened eagle. " TIME WILL TELL NOW" Look closely at your Promise Feathers."

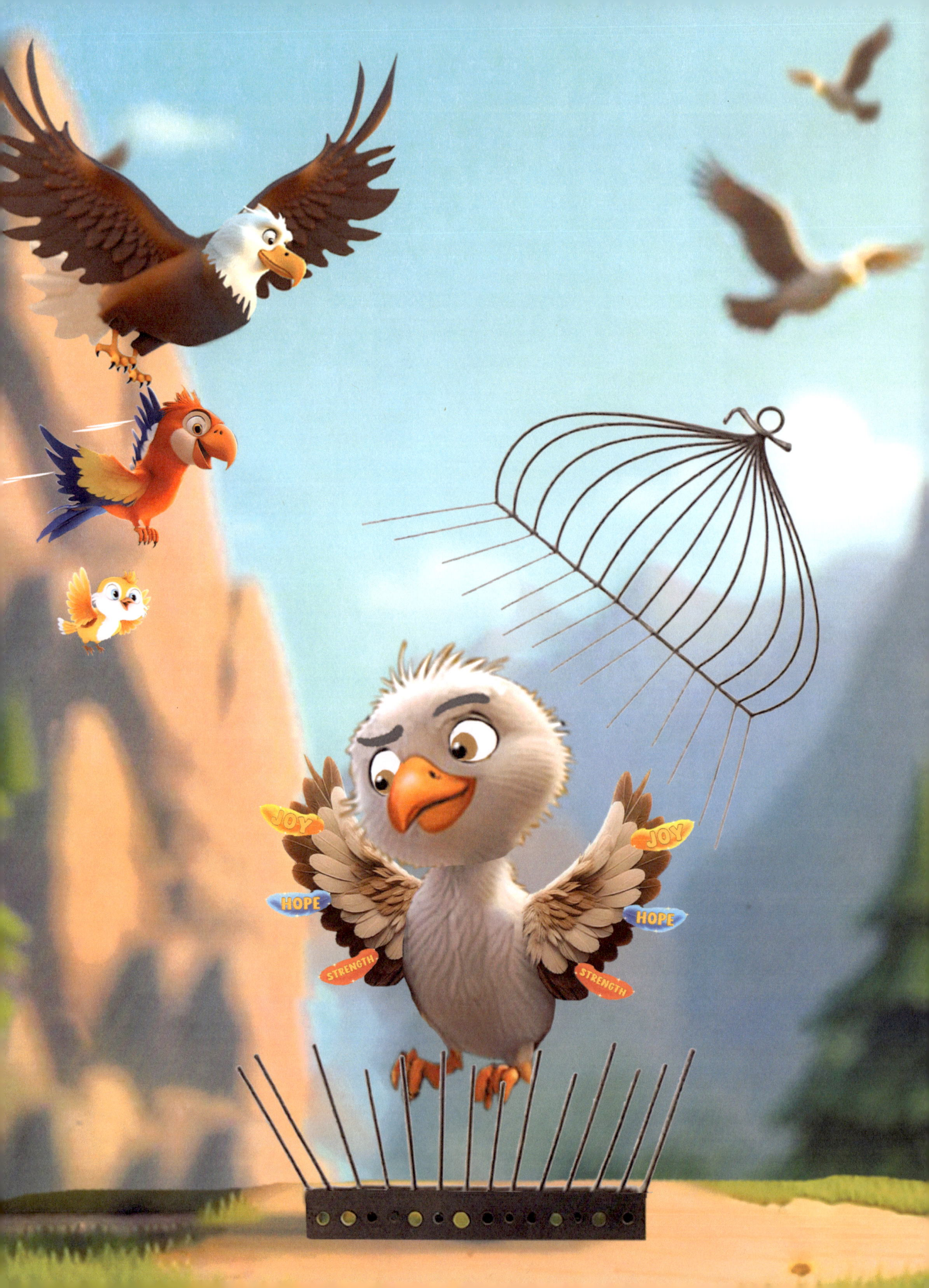
JOY
JOY
HOPE
HOPE
STRENGTH
STRENGTH

Looking at each feather carefully, Barry's Eyes widened "OH ! I GET IT NOW! I KNOW WHAT THE GOLD LETTERS MEAN."
"This Blue feather reads HOPE," he said "This Red feather reads STRENGTH" and " This yellow feather reads JOY. "WOW! HOPE, STRENGTH & JOY - That's the song in my heart. These were gifts sent with Wally, Kenny, & Harmony

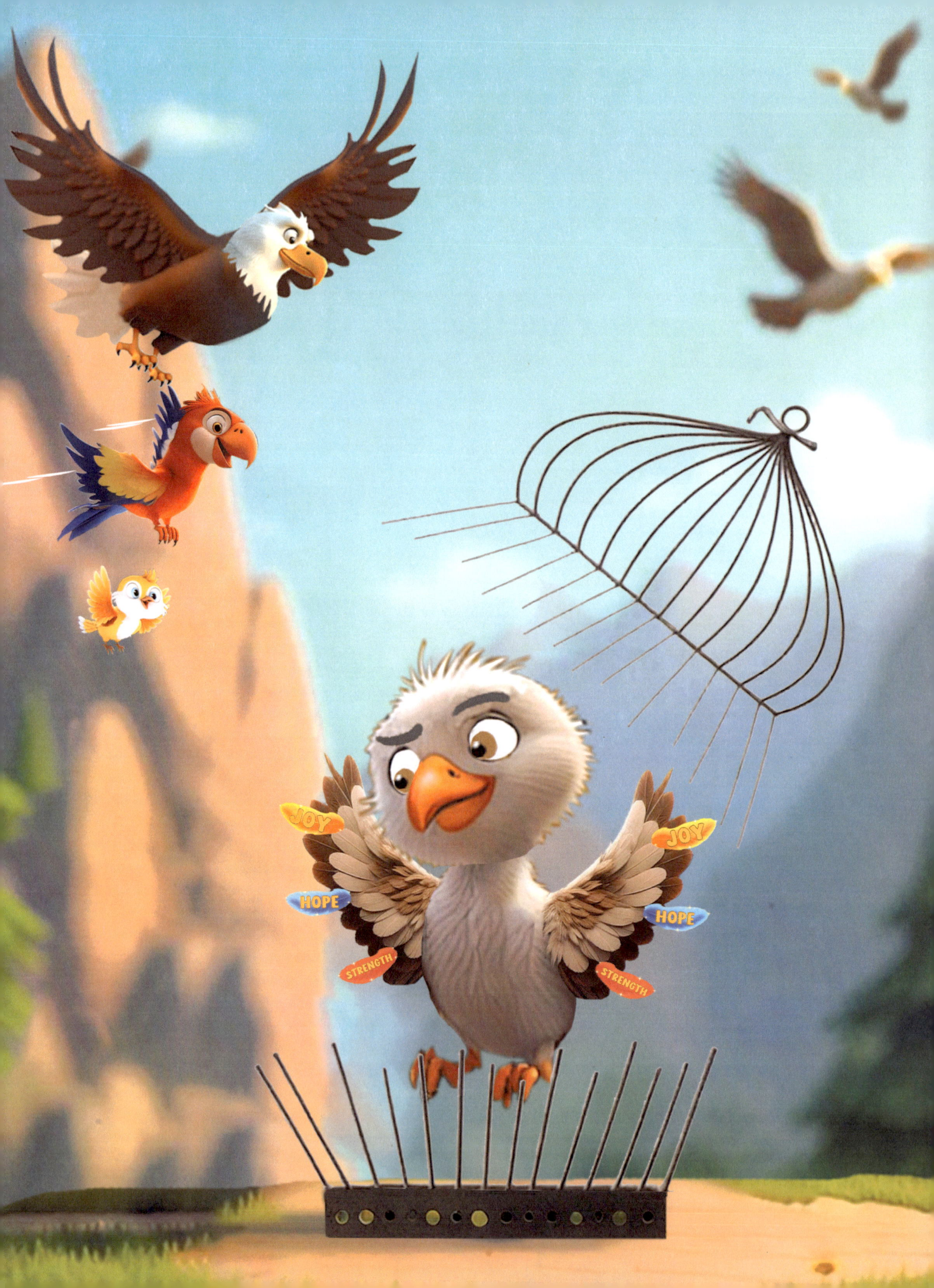
JOY
JOY
HOPE
HOPE
STRENGTH
STRENGTH

Barry shouted "All this time Wally, Kenny & Harmony came to show me how Truly loved I am. " Love makes all things possible, it never fails Barry thought.
Love showed me who I was meant to be, this kind of love changes you.
YES !!!!
I'M AN EAGLE
&
"Oh! My…..I Can Fly!"
OFF BARRY FLEW

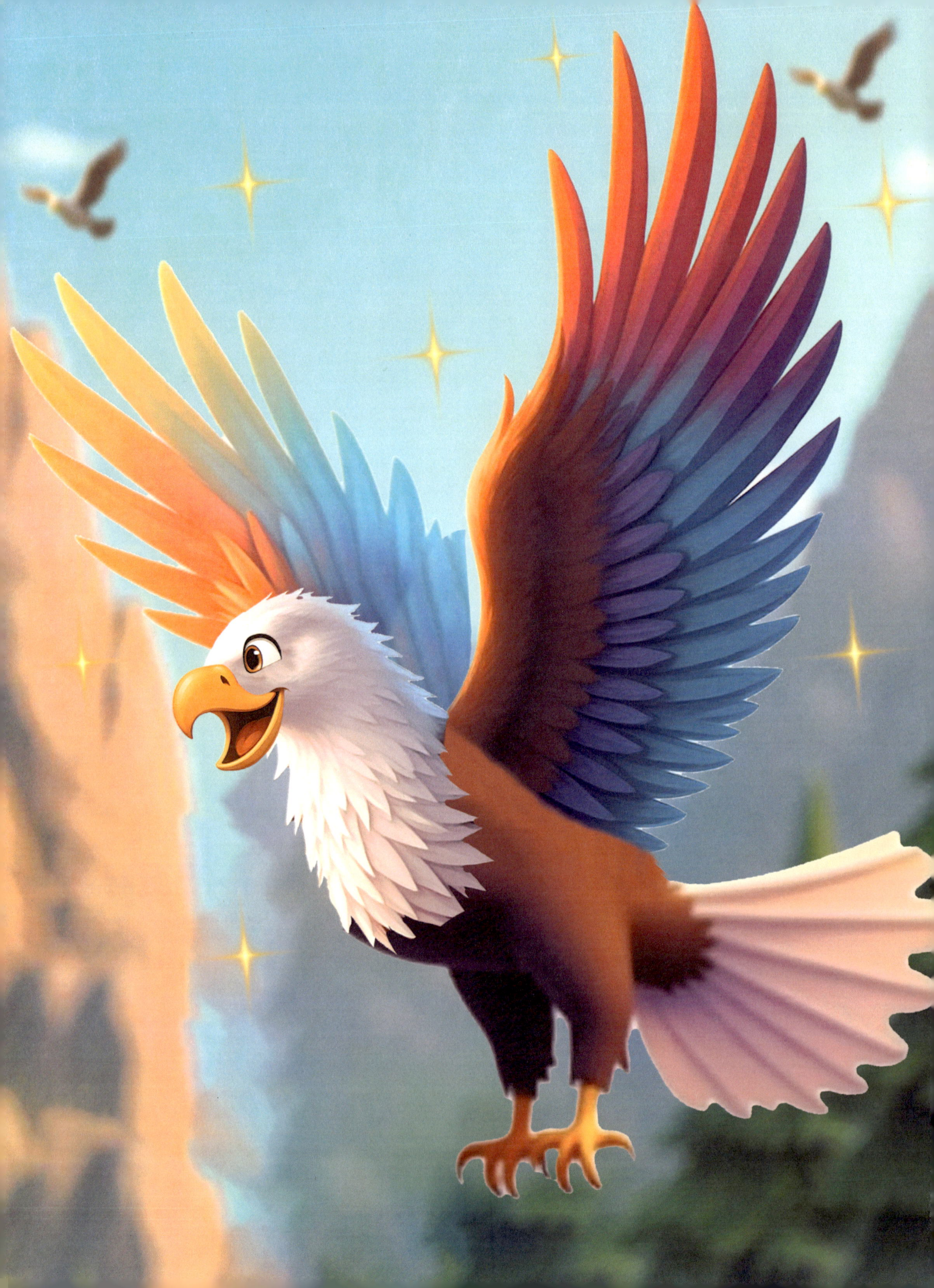

Barry became the most beautiful eagle in the sky, helping others find hope, strength and joy— Bringing a song for their hearts. He knew his mission: " It's my turn now. I'll help others know true love and show them who they were meant to be. The End !

1. What was Barry's dream to do? What do you dream to do?
2. Who were Barry's friends who came to help him? Who will help you?
3. Are you afraid to try something new?
4. What does it feel like to be different?
5. What bird to like the best? Why?